D0409077
WITHDRAWN

STARRING Jules
(IN DRAMA-RAMA)

BETH AIN

Illustrated by Anne Keenan Higgins

Scholastic Press / New York

Library of Congress Cataloging-in-Publication Data

Ain, Beth Levine.
Starring Jules (in drama-rama) / Beth Ain ; illustrated by Anne Keenan Higgins.
p. cm. — (Starring Jules ; 2)
Summary: Jules, excited and nervous about her part in a sitcom pilot, is also concerned about her class moving up ceremony and her touchy relationships with ex-best friend Charlotte and new best friend Elinor — it is almost too much drama for one seven-year-old New Yorker to handle.
ISBN 978-0-545-44354-8 (alk. paper)
1. Acting — Auditions — Juvenile fiction. 2. Best friends — Juvenile fiction. 3. Friendship — Juvenile fiction. 4. Elementary schools — Juvenile fiction. 5. New York (N.Y.) — Juvenile fiction. [1. Acting — Fiction. 2. Auditions — Fiction. 3. Best friends — Fiction. 4. Friendship — Fiction. 5. Elementary schools — Fiction. 6. Schools — Fiction. 7. New York (N.Y.) — Fiction.] I. Higgins, Anne Keenan, ill. II. Title.
PZ7.A
813.6 — dc23
2012041838

Designed by Natalie C. Sousa

12 11 10 9 8 7 6 5 4 3 2 1 13 14 15 16 17 18/0

Printed in the U.S.A. 23
First printing, September 2013

for

SKYLAR

and

AUTUMN

(as my dazzling nieces)

Lights! Camera! Action!

Read along as Jules Bloom's star continues to rise:

Starring Jules (as herself)
Starring Jules (in drama-rama)

CONTENTS

spy codes, movie-star bones, and other things that get cracked

"Six, seven, eight, nine —!" Elinor is counting the seconds until our handstand contest collapses.

"Jules!" Big Henry slams into the room and *crash!* Elinor and I are down in a heap.

"Big Henry!" I shout from our pileup. "I was going for the record! That was going to be my longest handstand ever." I turn to Elinor. "Right? I think we were going to get to ten seconds."

"Definitely," Elinor says, rubbing her arm. "But now I think I need a hospital. Is it serious?" She holds out her arm for my examination. Elinor is sometimes dramatic about small injuries, which I like very much because she is never dramatic about one other thing. Besides, when she says things like this, in her lovely Elinor of London accent, it sounds like *she* is the actress and I am the regular person, and I picture my best friend, Elinor, dressed up in a glittery gown and waving to people on a long red carpet, and I am one of those celebrity newscasters asking her about her earrings and her shoes —

"Jules!" Big Henry has come face-to-face with me, interrupting our imaginary moment. I look my little brother in the eyes and he doesn't blink. This must be serious.

I put my hands on his shoulders. "What is it?" I ask.

"Rick Hinkley cracked his leg," Big Henry says.

I gasp.

"Rick Hinkley cracked his leg?" I say.

"Is that spy code?" Elinor asks.

"What does this mean?" I ask Big Henry.

"Ask Mommy," he says.

"Hello?" Elinor asks. "Non-spy here. Please explain."

"Rick Hinkley is the star of *The Spy in the Attic*," I say.

Now Elinor gasps.

I run to the kitchen, where my mom is still on the phone. Today is Monday and tomorrow is supposed to be DAY ONE of being Lucy Lamb, spy-girl in the mega movie *The Spy in the Attic*, starring Mr.

Rick Hinkley, an actor who used to be a professional hockey player, but who is now a big-time movie star. I get to be out of school all morning tomorrow, which is why I am having a Monday afternoon playdate with Elinor when I would usually be sitting at the bar of my dad's almost-open restaurant, BLOOM!, doing my homework.

Standing in the kitchen with a phone to her ear, my mom holds up a finger to me before I can even say one word. "Is that Colby Kingston?" I whisper as loud as I can.

She nods. Colby Kingston has gone from being a primo casting director to being my mom's best friend. (I say *primo* partly because she likes the way I make up songs in diner booths and partly because she's the nicest, coolest tall-icy-drink-drinking person I've ever known. And yes, a little bit because she made me into an actress.) They spend a lot of time talking on the phone about things that have nothing to do with *The Spy in the Attic*, the movie in which I have twenty-two lines that I have been rehearsing every morning and night since the day I did not become the Swish (horrible orange-tasting) Mouthwash for Kids girl, and the movie that is now maybe, probably not going to happen because of Rick Hinkley's cracked-up leg.

Finally, my mom hangs up the phone.

"What?" I say.

"Well, Rick Hinkley broke his leg," my mom tells me. "But Jules, this is not the end of the world. Movies get postponed all the time."

"Postponed?" I ask. I am hoping *postponed* means pushed forward.

"Pushed back," my mom says.

I am having so many feelings inside my body that I feel like a pan of shake-over-the-stovetop popcorn. I can't even see my mom's face. I only see the tinfoil getting bigger and bouncier with all those thousands of kernels popping to life inside until it just explodes.

"Are you thinking about popcorn?" my mom asks.

I squint my eyes at her. I have been practicing squinting my eyes at people for my spy-girl role. “How did you know that?” I ask in my spy-girl voice.

“Because this is the kind of thing that usually makes you feel like you might explode stove-popped popcorn everywhere,” she explains.

I sit down on the floor and rest my head in my hands. Elinor and Big Henry come and sit next to me.

"So, what happens now?" Elinor asks.

I shrug.

"What happens now is we wait until Rick Hinkley's leg heals, and in the meantime, we get back to life as usual," my mom says.

"Life as usual is boring," I say. "Life as usual is all school, playdate, dinner, bed — boring! And then when school is over it will be camp, dinner, bed — boring!" I throw my hands in the air and start stomping back and forth. "And anyway, I'm probably going to forget my lines and then have to learn them again, which is —" I look at Big

Henry. "Hank?" I say in a big, loud director voice. Calling him Hank seems like something a director would do.

"BORING!" he yells.

"See? Even Big Henry knows," I say. "I rest my case."

"Jules!" my mom says. She looks like she's going to say something important, or like she might be very mad at me for freaking out like this, so I cover my ears. But instead she just looks at me for an extra-long minute and then she leaves the room.

"Where'd she go?" Elinor asks.

"Maaaaahmmy!" Big Henry yells in his whining four-year-old voice.

"Coming," she sings back.

"She's mad that I said life as usual is boring," I say.

"She doesn't sound mad," Elinor says.

"Trust me," I say. "She's mad."

"It seems like you're the one who's mad," Elinor says.

"She's dramatic," Big Henry says.

"Hank!" I say. Then I turn to Elinor, who looks upset. "Why do you look that way?"

"I don't like all the yelling," she says.

"You don't ever yell?" I ask.

"No," she says.

"Not ever? Not even in a good way, like a hooting-and-hollering-at-a-Yankees-game way?"

"Nope," Elinor says.

I study my new best friend and wonder

why, even though she looks like a regular, happy-on-the-outside person, she seems just the littlest bit sad on the inside.

Some crashing sounds come from the pantry-studio where my mom works, and we all look around the corner, but it isn't my mom who comes back through the door. It is her giganto easel, which she pushes all the way through the kitchen and into the living room. Ugly Otis looks up at the ruckus from his big dog bed in the corner and decides to join the sitting-on-the-floor crowd.

"There!" my mom pants. She seems proud. Elinor and I look at each other. We have been best friends for three full months now and she still forgets that my mom gets mad in different ways than her mom gets mad. Leona Breedlove, Elinor's mom, gives Elinor time in a naughty chair if she does something bad. And I only know this because Elinor told me, not because Elinor has ever done anything bad enough to actually get her into a naughty chair, since I think she is the best-behaved seven-year-old that has ever lived in New York City.

"Welcome to the show *Who Did That Fabulously Un-Boring Thing?*"

"The what?" Big Henry asks.

My mom is less of a naughty-chair punisher and more of a game-show punisher.

"It's a game, Hank," my mom says. She has gotten tired of calling my brother Big Henry all the time and now calls him Hank. She thinks it sounds strong and to the point, like Big Henry. She writes in a fat marker on the paper: *ROUND ONE*. Then she gets a serious expression and says, "Who turns

boring old milk into fizzy-ice-cream-cone milk with only a cup and a straw?"

"Jules does!" Big Henry yells.

"She does?" my mom — I mean the game-show host — asks. "Well, I don't know about that. That doesn't sound very boring at all, but all right, one point for Hank." She flips the page on the easel and writes *ROUND TWO*. "Who can turn boring old mud into a dee-luxe, state-of-the-art worm swimming pool?"

"Jules can!" Elinor says, getting up on her knees. She goes right back to sitting quietly and looking serious, like the shouting never happened. She seemed so, so happy for that little burst of a second that I decide that I am going to make my not-a-movie-star life be about getting Elinor to let out some hoots and hollers. Not just letting them out, but letting them stay out. That'll get her all cheered up.

"Are you sure, Elinor?" my mom asks. "Building a worm swimming pool doesn't sound even a little bit boring."

"I'm definitely sure," Elinor says.

"Oh, and just one more question — a bonus round," my mom says. "Which neurotic second grader managed to land herself the un-boring-est new best friend in new-best-friend history?"

Elinor smiles at this. "I don't see how anyone could get bored in this house for even one second." I am frustrated that Elinor thinks this is loads of fun, but at least she seems happy, which is a start.

"Fine," I say. "I'm sorry. Life is not boring. Only boring people get bored. I get it."

My mom claps and cheers WAY too loud,

and all of her crazy behavior is making my face feel hot. I want it to stop. "ANYWAY," I shout as loud as I can, "I already thought of a new project."

"First, watch the tone of your voice, Jules Bloom," my mom says. "You're on thin ice after that little display a minute ago."

"Sorry," I say.

"And second, is your new project boring?" she asks.

"Not at all," I say.

"Well, what is it?" Elinor asks.

"Nope, not telling. I may not be starting the movie tomorrow, but I am still a super-secret-spy-girl-in-training, you know. You'll find out soon enough."

Just then, the door opens and my dad walks in. "Hello!" he says.

"Daddy!" Big Henry and I yell as we run into my dad's arms.

"Rick Hinkley has a cracked-up leg and the movie is postponed, and Mommy did a game show to remind me that life is not boring," I say.

"And Jules has a new project!" Big Henry says.

"Elinor," my dad says seriously, "is all of this true?"

"Every last word, Mr. Bloom," Elinor says.

"Well, I have some news, too," he says. "The restaurant is in full bloom." We are all quiet for a minute.

“More spy codes?” Elinor asks.

“No!” I say. “Well, yes, it means BLOOM! has passed inspection!”

My dad hasn’t even gotten to cook in his own restaurant yet because of all the other things a chef needs to do before a restaurant can actually open.

“Yeth!” Big Henry’s lispy *yes* makes me laugh, and I start to hoot and holler Yankees-game style. We all do. All except Elinor, who smiles, but does not hoot and holler, or jump up and down. I have to fix this. I feel those butterflies start to flit around in my stomach, because soon enough there will be hooting and hollering coming out of Elinor, and I’m the only one who knows it.

early-morning ailments, un-boring berries, and new career opportunities

I wake up with a giant pain in my stomach. "Mommy!" I yell, which does not bring my mom, but it does bring my brother.

"What, Jules?" he says with his hands asking the question, like a grown-up. Sometimes I think Big Henry is more like a parent than a little boy. "Tell Mommy I have a Charlotte-ache," I say.

Big Henry leaves and I pull the covers over my head and wait.

"A Charlotte-ache?" my mom says, standing over my head. She has not yet pulled the covers off of me, and I know it's coming. I nod.

"So, we're talking about a stomachache, right?" she asks.

I nod again.

"A stomachache because you have to go to school and tell Charlotte that movie rehearsals aren't starting today after all?"

I nod again and I can't believe she hasn't pulled the covers off yet. I feel like I might suffocate. I picture the ocean in Florida

and getting sucked away by the undertow and I start to panic. I sit straight up and throw the covers off of me. "Why didn't you pull off my covers? I WAS DROWNING!" I say in a very loud voice, louder than my mother is comfortable with.

"Excuse me?" she says in her about-to-freak-out voice.

I start to cry. "She is going to make fun of me," I say. My ex–best friend, Charlotte (Stinkytown) Pinkerton, is just waiting for me to fail at being an actor. "And then she is going to tell me that she knows Hollywood and that this means there will be no movie and that I will never be a movie star and that at least it was nice while it lasted." I am hiccupping because the tears have turned my stomach upside down.

"Okay, calm down," my mom says, sitting on my bed and putting both of her hands on my head. "It sounds like you already know what Charlotte is going to say."

"So?"

"So that means you can prepare what you want to say right now, so you don't have to feel terrible when she says these things."

"What should I say?" I ask, knowing that she will not tell me.

"What do you want to say?" she asks. I knew it.

"That the movie is so going to happen and that broken bones heal fast, especially when you are part hockey star and part movie star," I say.

"Is that it?"

"And that it gives me time to work on my own secret project," I say.

"Okay," my mom says. "Good then. All set?"

I think for a minute. The Charlotte-ache seems to be over. I nod. "I guess so," I say.

"Great," she says. "So put on something very un-boring and I will make you an un-boring breakfast parfait of yogurt and granola and blueberries."

"Wow, that is very un-boring," I say, feeling much better.

I gobble up my parfait and head out into the heat wave, where even the bright, beautiful flowers sitting in their water pots at the deli on the corner look worn-out from holding up all this heavy air. Thankfully, the hot gets knocked right out of me by the blast of freezing-cold air that hits me in the face as I hop up the M104 stairs and find a seat. My mom chats with the bus driver while I stare at my goose bumps and Big Henry rides the bus roller-coaster style the rest of the way down Broadway.

The inside of my classroom feels more like the inside of an oven and I wonder why there can't be an in-between temperature during a heat wave. "Hola, Ms. Leon," I say to the best teacher that has ever taught in any school ever.

"Hola, Jules," she says back. I search the room for Elinor, but she isn't here yet. Even seeing my other friend Teddy would make me feel better, but he is late, as usual.

"How about an *hola* to the rest of us,

1 2 3 4 5 6 7 8
Aa Bb Cc

Jules?" Charlotte asks. "You weren't even supposed to be here today."

Charlotte has a way of being mean without actually *saying* anything mean.

"Well, movies get postponed all the time," I say.

"Is it because of Rick Hinkley's broken leg?" she asks.

"How do you know about that?" I say. I am not at all happy that Charlotte knows something about my life that I just found out myself.

"It was on the news last night, Jules. Everyone knows. They said it could be months until it heals."

Months! I think to myself. I try to remain calm. I try to remember what my mom said this morning, but I can't. I can't think of anything to say. Not one word.

"That's all right. Jules already has a new top secret project," Elinor says, throwing her backpack into her cubby. "Don't you, Jules?"

"Well, it's just my own project," I say. I wish I hadn't made a big deal about this, since it's kind of private and since it has to do with Elinor, and since I don't think Elinor would be happy if anyone knew it was about her, even if she doesn't know herself.

"So, you are taking a break from being a movie star to work on your own project when you have never even been in one movie yet?" Charlotte asks.

"That's right," I say. It seems like this is annoying to Charlotte, so I go with it.

"Correct," Elinor says.

I try not to let it bother me that Charlotte went right back to being a little bit mean to me after she was so nice about my Swish audition. I try to remember that we are not best friends anymore and that I have a wonderful new best friend who is never, ever mean, not even by accident.

"Do you know what movie stars do when no one wants them to be seen in an actual movie anymore?" Charlotte asks.

"What?" I ask.

"Aha! Sixty seconds to get rid of it!" Abby says, and she and Charlotte and Brynn all laugh their heads off.

"I don't play the *what* game," I say to the ABC's.

"It's not a game, Jules. It's life," Charlotte says.

"Fine," I say.

"Anyway," Charlotte says, "my Hollywood uncle says that most actors want to direct movies after they're finished acting in them. Then they get to tell everyone what to do, for once. So, what's your top secret plan, Jules?"

"My top secret project is . . ." I change my voice to a very, very quiet whisper, "SOMETHING I WILL NOT EVER TELL YOU."

"What?" Charlotte says, extra loud because she is so frustrated.

Elinor and I smile at each other. "Got rid of it pretty fast that time," I say.

"Class!" Ms. Leon says. "Time for morning writing. But before we begin, I have an announcement."

There is nothing better than the few seconds before an announcement. Ms. Leon will probably just say that we are supposed to bring in all box tops by Friday, but for this one second before she says that, I picture the word *ANNOUNCEMENT* all lit up behind Ms. Leon, and then I picture her saying, "*Charlotte Pinkerton, you've learned all you can for this year, so pack up your backpack and we'll see you next year!*" I know very well she won't say this, but at least for a few seconds I get to pretend the announcement has nothing at all to do with box tops.

"I have decided that for this year's moving-up ceremony we will put on a little show. ¡*Un espectáculo!*"

Everyone starts moving in their chairs and I look around to see a lot of excited faces. "We start rehearsing tomorrow."

An idea pops right into my head and comes flying out of my mouth as I shoot my hand in the air. "I want to be the director!" This is the first time in my whole life I have ever raised my hand without making extra sure I knew exactly what would come out of my mouth.

I feel everyone's eyes on me, but especially Charlotte's. "I am surprised to hear this, Jules!" Ms. Leon says. "I thought you were a budding actress."

"I am," I say, my face heating up the way it does. "But, I think I would like this, too."

"Thank you for telling me, but we'll figure it out tomorrow. For now, we write!"

We all pull out our notebooks and I have a list written as fast as ever, guarding my paper the way Charlotte showed me so she will not see one single word.

Reasons Why I Should Be the Director of the Moving-Up-Ceremony Show:

1. I would get to boss Charlotte and the ABC's around.

2. I would get to make Elinor hoot and holler for real so she will not be sad-serious anymore — top secret mission accomplished!

3. I would not have to act in front of my whole class and their whole families, since the entire idea of speaking in front of people I actually know makes

me more nauseous than orange mouthwash.

There — morning list completed. *El espectáculo* is the greatest thing that's happened since my morning parfait!

pilots without airplanes, doggie dance-offs, and zipped-up lips

Usually I wake up in the morning to the sound of Big Henry's giant feet coming down the hallway, or to giant, Stinkytown-sized stomachaches like I did yesterday. But today, I wake up when the phone rings. A very early morning phone call could mean any number of things. A list!

Things That Could Happen When the Phone Rings:

1. You could become a movie star.

2. You could find out you are not going to be a movie star for at least another three months.

3. You could find out your food delivery has arrived.

I hear my mom say, "Oh, hi, Colby!" in a very cheerful way. It sounds like she is not mad at Colby for calling to postpone the movie. I wish I were not mad at Colby, either, since it isn't her fault that Rick Hinkley broke his leg. But I am.

I hop out of bed and get right to the kitchen, where my mom is flinging around a knife with cream cheese on it.

"You are kidding," my mom says.

"What?" I say.

She holds up that finger again. The same one from Monday. "Oh, wow, Colby," my mom says, and she is smiling so big I think I might burst. I start jumping up and down and waving my hands in the air.

"WHAT IS 'OH, WOW'!?" I say at the top of my lungs.

"Hold on a sec, Colby," my mom says,

covering up the phone with her hand. "There is a pilot being shot here in New York, and believe it or not, they need a little girl to replace the other little girl who was supposed to be in the pilot."

I blink my eyes at my mom. I have no words to describe what I am feeling. My mom is still smiling, which confuses me, so I have to ask, "A little girl and a pilot got shot?"

My mom puts the phone down on the counter. "I am so sorry, Jules," she says, sitting me down at the table. "*Pilot* is another word for the first show in a series, like the shows you watch on TV sometimes."

This news is getting better. "Go on," I say.

"So, there is a show like that being shot — er, filmed — right here in New York City, which is unusual because most shows like that are filmed in California."

"Hollywood?" I ask, proud that I know there is a Hollywood in California that is famous for moviemaking, and not for card games on the beach like the Hollywood in Florida, where Grandma Gilda lives.

"Right," she says. "And this is only a pilot episode of a sitcom —"

"What's a sitcom?" I ask.

"It stands for *situation comedy.* It just means that any problems that come up usually get resolved in thirty minutes, and in a funny way," she says.

"That's sounds wonderful," I say.

"Great," my mom says. "Now, the network — the people who decide what will be on TV — may or may not even like the show. We won't know for a little while. But for the moment, Colby has convinced them to cast you as the little sister, and you don't even have to audition because they don't have the time, and they trust Colby, and they saw your Swish audition tape and the tape of your rehearsal with Rick Hinkley, and they said yes!" My mom seems more excited about this than she was about *The Spy in the Attic.*

"I am going to be on TV?" I ask.

"Maybe," she says.

I jump up now and pull my mom out of her chair and we dance "Ring Around the Rosy" style until Big Henry and Ugly Otis come running in, and then I say, "I am going to be in a sitcom, on TV!" and Big Henry goes crazy and my mom takes his hands and I take Ugly Otis's big paws and we dance like this for another minute before my mom remembers something and runs back to the phone.

"Colby?" she says, laughing. "I am so sorry!"

Colby says something.

"Yes," my mom says. "She's in."

She hangs up the phone and looks at me.

"What?" I ask.

"Is that what you're wearing to school?" she asks.

I look down at my flannel nightgown and I picture myself riding the M104 in it. And then I picture the bus-driver lady shaking her head at me. "I don't think so," I say.

My mom laughs and I go to my room to get changed. I hear Big Henry ask my mom, "Is Jules wearing that nightgown to school?"

"No, Hank," my mom says. "Are you wearing your dinosaur rain boots to school?"

"Yeth," he says.

"I thought so," she says.

It hasn't rained in weeks.

At school, I see Teddy and Elinor before I see anyone else. Perfecto!

"Guess what?" I say.

They look at each other. I can see that neither one of them wants to say "*What?*" because of Charlotte and the ABCs' ridiculous sixty-seconds-to-get-rid-of-the-word-*what* rule.

"Say '*What?*' " I say. "I dare you!"

"What?" they both say at the same exact time, laughing.

"Jinx!" they both say again, laughing even harder.

"Excellent," I say, trying on that game-show-host voice my mom used. "You jinxed at the exact same time. Neither one of you has to stop talking." I think about this for a second. "Actually, both of you have to stop talking."

They both close their mouths tight, zipping them up with their fingers. "I might get to be on TV," I say. I watch my friends' faces. They don't move their mouths, but their eyes get big. "I am going to be in a pilot, which my mom told me is just another name for the first show in a series, and aren't you guys glad she told me that?"

They both nod again, their eyes popping out even more. "Otherwise, Charlotte would have gotten all crazy know-it-all, making fun of me for thinking that my mom had told me a pilot was getting shot when she just meant they were filming a show." I look at their faces. I can't take the quiet for one more second.

"Elinor and Teddy, Elinor and Teddy, Elinor and Teddy!" I say as fast as I can, releasing them from the jinx. They both burst out with laughter.

"How did this happen so fast?" Elinor asks.

"Another girl was supposed to play the little sister but now she can't for some reason and they needed someone fast and Colby Kingston told them about me," I explain. I picture Colby shaking hands and throwing her head back and doing all those tall-icy-drink things she does and I am not even a little bit mad at her anymore.

"Oh my goodness, the stars are aligning!"

Elinor says. "Don't you see?" she says. "Rick Hinkley's leg got broken, which made Jules upset, but free! And then something happened to another girl at the very same time, but luckily . . . LUCKILY, Jules was free to take her spot, and now Jules Bloom is going to be on the television!"

"TV is not better than movies," Teddy says. But then he looks at me. "But it is cool." I think he says this because he doesn't want me to push him, which I sometimes do when he spends too much time being smart and not enough time being fun. "But aren't you nervous? This is the kind of thing that usually makes you imagine crazy things happening, like you trying to be the

sassy little sister, but instead of being sassy, you are spazzy and you just say and do a lot of spazzy things."

I push him, after all.

"See?" he says. "Spazzy."

Charlotte walks in then and throws her

backpack into her cubby and flops down into her chair. We all look at each other. "What's the matter, Charlotte?" Elinor asks in her polite, Elinor way.

"There is nothing the mattah, Elinoh," Charlotte says, trying to mimic Elinor's accent and doing it kind of well, actually. Elinor's cocoa skin gets red in a way I have never seen and I am furious at Charlotte for this.

"Charlotte," I say, my heart pounding so loud my voice echoes in my ears, "just because you are in one of your moods does not mean you can spread it all around. Elinor was being nice."

Charlotte doesn't look at me. She just

looks straight ahead like she is imagining we are not there.

Ms. Leon claps us all into our seats and I forget about Charlotte's temper tantrum while I wait to hear more about *el espectáculo*! "The show needs to be very simple since we only have a couple of days to work on it. And it should show your families something important about what we've learned this year. This is your writing assignment for this morning: What have you learned this year? From this, we will decide about our show."

I get writing right away. This is going to be my longest list yet.

☆ ☆ ☆ ☆ ☆

It is almost dinnertime and I am in the middle of doing my reading comprehension homework when Big Henry barges in. "The sitcom is here!"

Sitcom is Big Henry's new favorite word ever since this morning. My mom hands me a piece of paper.

"It's a treatment," she says. "That means a summary of the show. You won't see the script until the read-through tomorrow. I'll pick you up from school a little early."

"Oh," I say. I look at the page quickly. At the top it says, *Treatment for LOOK AT US NOW!* I read it, and this is what I comprehend from it:

1. The Summers family is very wealthy. I decide wealthy is a good vocabulary word. I think it means rich.

2. There are three Summers children — a boy-crazy teenage girl, a bossy boy, and a meddling but cute little sister. They go to a fancy private school, and they drive around the city in a car, which no one in real life does, unless you are a taxi driver.

3. They used to be a regular family, who lived in a regular-sized

apartment, but then Mr. and Mrs. Summers won a TV singing contest and now they are world famous and never home. I decide this is why the show is called *Look at Us Now!*

I am so excited, I can hardly get through the rest of my reading comprehension, but I do, because I know that my parents' rule about acting is that school comes first — no matter how exciting it is to think about meeting my TV family tomorrow. No matter how much I want to rush through the whole rest of tonight, and the whole day of school tomorrow, just so I can start to be the sitcom version of me.

So I do my homework perfectly, checking my work more than once because I don't like to be wrong on reading comprehension, since the answers are basically right in front of you. Then I race through dinner, and I do not take one extra second brushing my teeth. I even read Big Henry a superhero book without him begging me to, so that he will go to bed faster, which means I can go to bed faster, since he needs to be asleep before I can turn on my book on tape, which is *Pippi Longstocking*.

When I finish reading to Big Henry, he says, "Can I be on your sitcom?" Before I can answer, he spots his 3-D glasses next to his bed, puts them on, and turns off his bedside light.

"You can't be on the show, Hank," I say, looking at my silly brother lying there in

the dark with 3-D glasses on, listening to Paddington Bear. "But you probably should be."

And it's true. Every sitcom should probably have a Big Henry in it.

fake soccer, laundry lists, and how to connect the dots

It is already tomorrow, which I thought would never come all night long when I couldn't sleep, because being excited about the sitcom turned into being nervous right after I put Big Henry to bed. I started thinking about how Big Henry would be perfect on a sitcom and how he wouldn't be nervous or shy because he just says and does funny things on purpose. I only say or do funny things by accident, and usually because I am nervous. And then I started to think about Teddy calling me spazzy instead of sassy and, well, I'm pretty sure I didn't fall asleep until exactly one second before I heard my mom telling me it was time to get up.

Now I have to spend the whole morning at school finding a way to get back to being excited — only excited. Then I remember that instead of having to watch a bunch of four-year-olds play fake soccer in the nursery-school gym after school, I get to take a taxi with my mom. A taxi! I am feeling mighty excited by the time I get to school, and before I know it, it's lunchtime.

"I am very pleased to see that most of you understand that we have spent a lot of time this school year learning about our community," Ms. Leon says after lunch. I am surprised she has already read our lists since I think mine was at least twenty numbers long.

"I can see that you know the boroughs of New York City, you know where the Statue of Liberty is, and you know where City Hall is. It seems like you also know some math facts, some science facts, and that you even liked writing about small moments." I am waiting for her to mention something I wrote on my list. "I also learned from your lists that our classroom is like a little city and that I am your mayor," she says now. I smile. That one is mine. "So I think it would be interesting if we told the story of our little classroom community through small moments. What are some of the small groups within our classroom community?" she asks the class.

"Helpers!" Brynn shouts out, which makes perfect sense, since Brynn spends a lot of time wiping the sink and picking up pencils off the floor.

Ms. Leon writes *helpers* on the board.

"Artists!" Abby says. I think of Abby lining up the markers and colored pencils in

FAMOUS WOMEN of Mathematics

1. Helpers

rainbow order. Pinks to purples to blues to greens — she always makes the supply drawer look like an art project.

"Scientists!" Teddy says. No explanation required.

"Entertainers!" Charlotte says, and she is smiling, which she never did once all day yesterday. But even so, it isn't the big smile she would usually have at a time like this.

No one yells anything for a minute.

"How about mathematicians?" Ms. Leon asks.

"Yes," Charlotte says. Charlotte loves math almost as much as she loves being the center of attention.

"Jules," Ms. Leon says, "please come forward." I am so nervous about my after-school activity that I forget to be nervous about walking to the front of the room. "What a show like this really needs is a narrator, and since you are an actress, I think you will do a fine job at it," Ms. Leon says. A narrator is very different from a director, I think, since a narrator has to actually speak out loud in front of real live people. "Jules will help connect the dots of the show, but her role is just as important as everyone else's role."

"So Jules is not the boss?" Abby asks.

"The only boss here is me," says Ms. Leon. Everyone laughs at this, except Charlotte, who still isn't paying attention to anything at all.

"Okay, try and put yourself in a category

here and don't worry if it isn't the only thing you're good at," Ms. Leon says.

I have no idea which of these groups I fit into, so I am especially glad to be the narrator right now, since it is very embarrassing when everyone is moving all around and you have no idea where you fit in. Everybody finds their way into a group, except Elinor. "Jules," Ms. Leon says, "why don't you work with Elinor to find a group?"

"Entertainers," I say without even thinking for one second. This is the group where there will be hooting and hollering, I think.

"Jules," Elinor says, "maybe maths?" Elinor says *maths* because that is what they say in London for *math*.

"Nah," I say. "Entertainers will be more fun."

"No," she says.

"What if I tell you it would help a lot with my supersecret side project?" I ask.

"How is that possible?" she asks.

"It just is," I say.

"Jules, there is no way I am going to be an entertainer. That's your thing," she says.

Until this second, I never ever not even once thought of myself as an entertainer, and I didn't realize I had a thing.

"Well, what's your thing, then?" I ask. "Is there *anything* that would make you happy?" When this comes out of my mouth, it sounds much meaner than it sounded when it was in my head.

Elinor shrugs and looks like she's going to cry, but she doesn't and I am relieved, because if I ever made Elinor cry, then I would cry, and everyone in the room would think we were a couple of crybabies. "Why don't I just be whatever you think I should be? That's pretty much the way things work, isn't it?"

Even though it sounds like Elinor is mad at me, I think she isn't. I think something is bothering her and maybe it's the same something that is making her sad, even when she seems happy. I want to talk to my mom about this, but it is only the afternoon and I have to get all the way through the rest of school and the whole entire read-through before I can talk to her about anything, and by then I will probably forget that this happened in the first place.

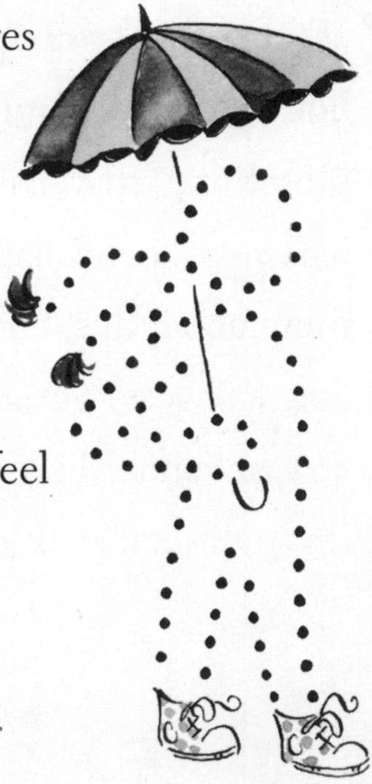

"Well, so just try out the entertainers and if it doesn't work, we'll think of something." I give her a little push in the direction of Charlotte. The two of them just stand there looking very unhappy together. I look around the room at all the groups and I try to picture myself as the line in one of those connect-the-dots pictures in dentist-office magazines. I picture dot after dot after dot, all trying to be one simple picture of a girl and her parasol, and I feel tired. This seems like a lot for one person to do.

Ms. Leon's voice has some good news. "Ah!" she says. "I forgot the best part . . . we are going to end our 'Small Moments in Our Community' skit with a big moment — a song from *The Sound of Music,* 'So Long, Farewell.' Our *espectáculo* needs a big finale!"

Yes, it does, I think. We have been learning these songs all spring in music class. The whole class lets out a cheer, even Charlotte and Elinor, the sad-face twins.

We practice for a while, and Ms. Leon helps us write down the small moment each group will talk about. I think this is basically another way of saying what we learned

"I don't want to be the main star, Jules," Elinor says. "Charlotte is pretty good at it, anyway."

"How about an apology, Jules?" Ms. Leon says.

"Sorry," I mutter to Charlotte, even though I am really not sorry, especially since Charlotte made Elinor take her side.

Charlotte looks right at me now. "You are not sorry. You just want to be in control of everything and Ms. Leon did NOT make you the director. You are just a narrator, not even an actress."

"All right," Ms. Leon says, and she claps her hands, which is kind of a Maria von Trapp thing to do. "That's enough for today," Ms. Leon says. "Jules and Charlotte, you both need to go home and think about how you are going to work together. We only have one and a half days left to practice."

"Why only one and a half?" I ask. I think we still have Friday and Monday.

"Monday is Field Day!" Ms. Leon says. She seems very happy about this.

"What's Field Day?" Elinor asks.

"It's a day filled with sports, sports, and more sports," Teddy says. Field Day is not Teddy's favorite day.

"And then we all get hosed down with freezing-cold water," I say. I hate this part.

"Wow," Elinor says, and she smiles this smile I have never seen on her before. Then she does this little jump in place, which she also never does, and it seems like Elinor is very excited about Field Day, which doesn't make any sense at all since the only good thing about Hippity Hop races in the crazy-hot heat is the giant watermelon slice they give you when it's all over.

Thankfully, the phone rings at this moment and it is for me.

"Jules," Ms. Leon says while I pack up my things, "we'll practice your introductions of each small moment when we go through the whole play tomorrow."

I grab my bag and walk slowly toward the office, where my mom is waiting for me. I am especially glad to see her since I don't feel very good about my fight with Charlotte.

"Excited?" she asks.

I shrug.

We hop in a cab and my mom is just about to turn off the TV that only runs ads and scary news broadcasts when I say, "Wait, don't!"

She looks at the screen and we laugh. At the very same time, we say, "It's Billy, the blond-haired, blue-eyed, bow-tie-wearing Swish boy!" We have no idea what Billy's real name is, but he just looks like a Billy, and he really is so good at being the Swish boy. It is hard to look away.

The ad ends, and Billy does not spit out

orange mouthwash all over the place like I did. He never does. Billy is perfect. I take off my rainbow sweatbands and press them against my eyes to hold back the tears. I want to turn this taxi around and go watch fake soccer instead.

dream families, scheduling conflicts, and the other New York City

"Jules," my mom says, "take those things off your eyes. We're here."

When I get out of the taxi, things are blurry because I am nervous, and also because I am blinded by rainbow-sweatband pressure, but I can see well enough to know we have arrived at a very pretty house on the Upper East Side, which I hardly ever go to since we mostly only know people who live on the West Side. I also don't know anyone who lives in an actual house — not an apartment — in the city, so I am very curious about this.

"Why aren't we going to a studio?" I ask as we walk up the steps to the front door.

"Colby told me that this show is based on the writer's real life and that they wanted the cast to do the read-through in his house so you would understand the show better." My mom looks at me. "Ready?"

I shrug again. My mouth is too dry to talk. I mash my sweatbands into a ball and squeeze the ball tight with my left hand, which makes me feel at least a little bit ready.

I find out three life-altering things the minute we walk into the dining room of the fanciest not-apartment I have ever seen:

1. Townhouses are not anything like apartments.

2. I get to miss school tomorrow because they want to do a full rehearsal before they shoot the pilot for real.

3. Billy the Swish boy is in the sitcom, too!

There are so many things going on in my head that I forget to be nervous for a minute. I smile and shake hands with everyone, and they are all so excited to meet me that I feel a little bit like a movie star! And then I meet Billy, whose name is not Billy. It is John McCarthy, which is kind of the opposite of Billy, if you think about it.

"Jordana!" I hear someone yell.

"What does everyone want?" I hear next, in a Southern accent, and then a tall teenage girl with blond curly hair comes over to us, looking at her phone the whole time. I would definitely walk into a wall if I tried to do this.

But Jordana doesn't walk into a wall. She just looks at me quickly and says, "I'm Jordana, but you can call me Sydney, which is my *Look at Us Now!* name, but don't get too used to *that* name since this show probably won't last either, and we'll all be someone else all over again." She says all of this in a super-sweet voice that somehow feels like the opposite of sweet. It is very, very quiet for a minute.

"Okay," John McCarthy says, clapping his hands together. "That was fun!"

His loud clap makes me blink that rainbow-sweatband blink, and I realize I have a question. "What is my name?" I ask. Everyone laughs. But the truth is, the treatment didn't have any names in it.

"You are Sylvie," John McCarthy says. "And I am Spencer, the mature older brother. Funny, right?"

LOOK AT US

"Hardly," Jordana says over her phone. Then she puts it down at her side for the first time. "Anyway, you might be older than Sylvie, but you are younger than Sydney."

"Middle child," John McCarthy says. "I can handle it." Then he nods big at my mom and they laugh, and I think I know what they are talking about but I'm not really sure, and none of it even matters because even though I am very afraid of Jordana and her phone and even though John McCarthy seems a little bit crazy . . . I KIND OF LOVE MY TV FAMILY.

We all sit down around a giganto table where there are scripts for each of us.

Jordana has the first line of the first episode. She says, "Sylvie, darling, would you mind getting me some tea?"

I think for a second that she is calling me *Sylvie Darling*, like *Darling* is my last name, and I am confused because I think our TV last name is Summers. Someone clears his throat and I snap out of it.

I am supposed to say, "*How about you get your own tea, Sydney, darling?*" which is something I would never really say in real life, and this makes the butterflies go flying around like crazy inside my body. I wish, wish, wish I could be Sylvie Darling — I mean Summers — instead of me.

I squeeze my rainbow-sweatband ball and say my line without stopping, but not with any sass because, well, because of the spaz situation. I am so worried that if I try to add any pizzazz at all, I will mess up, say a word wrong, or knock over someone's tall icy drink. I think I am not doing a very good job, since they hired me for this show all because I spit out Swish Mouthwash all over the place and sang a jingle, and they probably were hoping I'd do more than just sit around a very big table and read.

We read through the lines very quickly, and people are making scribbling notes all over their scripts and flipping pages back and forth and all I am doing is concentrating on not getting anything wrong. It gets to be my turn again and next to my name there is a word in parentheses. It says, (*sarcastically*). I think my heart stops beating. Everyone is looking at me to say my line, but I don't. I raise my hand instead,

and everyone laughs a little bit. My mom looks over at me and nods a lot. She is always happy when I raise my hand.

"I don't know what *sarcastically* means," I say.

"Really, Jules, you don't know what it means?" John McCarthy says really loud. "Great going!"

My heart stops beating again, AND my knees start shaking now.

"He's kidding, Jules!" Jordana says. "He's being sarcastic."

"Oh!" I say. And I think I understand but my knees never stop shaking the whole rest of the time, and the only thing I am very happy about is that the rest of the words in parentheses are words like (*with emotion*) and (*singing*).

"Nice job, everyone," the director says at last. I don't remember his name even though everyone has said it a million times. "We will make some changes for tomorrow, so be at the studio bright and early to read them through. And then we rehearse for real."

There are lots of good-byes that take a really long time, and all I want to do is get into my pajamas. Outside, we are back in the regular New York City, so when we get into a taxi, I open my window right away and look out at the street and look at everything in the pretty blue-gray light.

"You were really something today, Julesie," my mom says. "I can't believe how you read all those words and how you raised your hand like that. Did you have fun?"

"Kind of," I say. "But it was hard, too." I can't look at my mom. My eyes are burning.

"Jules, look at me. Are you okay?" she asks.

"I'm tired!" I yell. I do not like yelling at my mom, but sometimes I feel like my body doesn't have the energy not to yell.

"Hey," she says. "I'm going to give you a pass for that one because it's been a really long day, but being tired doesn't make it okay to talk like that."

"Sorry," I say, and I really mean it, but my *sorry* still sounds a little bit like a yell.

"Go ahead and look out the window," my mom says. Then she squeezes my hand until we get home.

☆ ☆ ☆ ☆ ☆

I feel much better after I get showered and into my pajamas. I am reading a just-right-for-my-reading-level book on the sofa when my mom says to my dad, "I heard that the Pinkertons are looking at houses on Long Island."

"What's Long Island?" I ask.

"It's a suburb," my dad says.

"What does that mean?" I ask.

"It means a regular place with cars and houses and backyards with jungle gyms, and basements underneath where kids can go and make all the mess they want," my mom says, smiling.

"And shopping malls," my dad says. "Lots and lots of shopping malls."

"Like Florida?" I ask.

"Yes," my mom says.

"Worse than Florida," my dad says.

"Robby!" my mom says. "Jules, don't listen to him. Daddy grew up on Long Island. You know this. He grew up in a nice town and now he likes living in the city because sometimes people like to do the opposite of what they are used to. Does that make sense?"

I can't think of any time when I don't want to do things exactly the way I always do them. "No," I say.

"Well, anyway, I'm sure wherever the Pinkertons move will be lovely. I'm sure with the baby, they've just had it with the city, and I can certainly understand that," she says.

I think my mom would like to go to a place with basements and backyards and my dad would definitely not, which is good, because the whole idea of changing something as big as where I live is just too much for me to even imagine.

"Teeth, Julesie," my mom says. But while I am brushing my teeth, I start to think about Charlotte moving to the suburbs, and then I try to picture my life without Stinkytown, which is a little bit impossible because I can't remember not knowing her. I feel tears behind my eyes and they burn and I don't want to cry, and I also smell the delicious smell of whatever my dad is cooking for grown-up dinner. Since he gets home too late to eat with us, I always have to wait until the next day to eat his creations.

I get under my covers and close my eyes and try to picture a basement, a magical place under the ground where you can hide and put on shows and make forts. I am interrupted by more garlicky smells coming from the hallway, and now all I can see is a glamorous restaurant with white tablecloths and clinking glasses and warm bread and pats of butter in the shape of seashells. I start to feel angry that all of this is going on without me.

I am supposed to wait for my mom to come and tuck me in, but I can't. So I take some baby steps into the living room, holding my nose.

"Jules, what are you doing?" my dad asks.

I shrug. This is what I do now when I don't have the right answer for something.

"I mean why are you holding your nose?" he asks.

"Because of the clinking glasses and the seashell butter and it just smells so good and I know you won't let me eat with you," I say. "And now I have to figure out how to be Sylvie and I have to figure out how to make Elinor hoot and holler and Charlotte might move to a place with basements and I will never even see her basement since we are not friends anymore!" I start to cry.

My mom looks at me. She is on the phone. She holds it out to me and I take it right away, since I know who is on the other end of that phone call.

I wait for Grandma Gilda to recognize my breathing.

"Eddie?" she says.

I nod. Our George and Eddie nicknames always make me feel better.

"Listen, I'm packing up my suitcase and hopping a flight in time for the moving-up show." I let out a big breath. "So, for now, just do what I do — positive affirmations. Look at the mirror and say, 'I am Jules Bloom and I can handle anything, even Stinkytown moving to the burbs.' "

I laugh because she called Charlotte *Stinkytown,* which is really not something grown-ups are supposed to do. "George," I say, "come soon."

"As fast as I can, Eddie," she says. I hand the phone back to my mom, and when I turn around, my dad has put down a placemat in front of my stool at the island. Then he puts down a small plate with a garlicky pile of stir-fried chicken and brown rice! I eat it all up slowly, and I try not to think about anything that's bothering me. Not the moving-up play, not the sitcom taping, not Charlotte moving. And definitely not the toothpaste taste in my mouth that is making the stir-fry taste more minty than I think it is supposed to be.

playing hooky, dancing on countertops, and other ways to shrug off real life

I wake up and am very happy that I have already met my TV family and that the read-through is over. Getting that over with made me more tired than any handstand contest I have ever done. I am also happy that I do not have to go to school and watch

Charlotte hog up the whole entertainers skit, while Elinor doesn't even come close to hooting and hollering.

I am very frustrated that my Elinor project hasn't worked out, and that just because Charlotte might move to a house with a basement, she is being more terrible than ever.

My mom and I run off to rehearsal at the studio this time, where they made a whole set that looks exactly like that fancy townhouse!

The first thing I start to understand today is that my TV family isn't just the other actors, it is all the people who help make the show. There are camera people, and lighting people, and the writers who make up what we say, and the writers who actually write our lines in very big handwriting on cards. They are kind of like a community, I think, like our classroom, or a city. Best of all, though, they are all funny and nice, which is especially good since today I need to actually act out all those words in parentheses, not just say them.

Besides that, my mom has taken an entire

day off of work and I know she is in the middle of putting together a big gallery show and I feel afraid that I will not be good at being Sylvie and *she* will be very frustrated.

I see Jordana sitting in a corner with earbuds in and her eyes closed, and then I see John McCarthy laughing his belly laugh with all the camera guys, and his mom is on the phone, chatting. Everyone seems like they know their place, like they belong here.

"Hi," my mom says, sitting down next to me.

"Hi," I say quietly.

"Are you nervous?" she asks.

"I'm afraid of Jordana," I say.

"She's a moody teenager," my mom says. "You probably should be afraid of her."

I laugh. "Let's talk about something else," I say.

"Like what?" she asks.

And then I remember! "Like, why does Elinor have to be sad? And why does she seem mad at me about it? All I did was try to get her into a hooting-and-hollering group for the moving-up skit, and she said, 'Fine. I'll just do what I'm told.' Or something like that."

"Hmmm," my mom says. "Sounds like something is bothering her."

"Well, yeah, but what? She's so perfect, I can't even imagine what could be wrong."

"I bet you could imagine if you really gave it some thought, Julesie. She just moved here all the way from London and she had to start a brand-new school in the middle of the year and there is an ocean in between her and her father, right?"

"Right," I say. "So she's homesick?"

"Maybe."

"But this is her home now," I say.

"Well, maybe she's having some trouble adjusting. Maybe she misses her dad. And maybe she feels like an outsider. Kind of the way you feel right now, maybe." I think about leaving New York City with only my mom and moving to a whole new country, and I think I would be horribly, grossly sick. I feel sorry for not knowing this about Elinor, but I don't even have a chance to think about how to fix it because there is a sitcom to put on.

"Okay, everybody — places!" The director says this and I realize now that I could not have been the moving-up-play director. You have to talk very loud to be a director. I would be one very red-hot-faced director. We spend a whole lot of time reading our lines over and over, and even though I get to like being Sylvie more and more, I don't think anyone thinks I'm doing a very good job. Here is why I think this:

1. There are a lot of takes when I say my lines. A take is like a do-over, and I love them. I wish I could use them in real life.

2. There is a lot of whispering after I say my lines, and I know it's the bad kind of whispering, like "she's not ANYTHING like Colby said she was" kind of whispering. And they are right.

3. I'm not anything like John McCarthy, who is just so good at acting and saying his funny lines that I even hear my mom laughing, and I'm definitely not like Jordana, who is very, very serious and scary, but who does a very good job of being Sydney. Such a good job that I forget

she's serious and scary when I'm doing a scene with her.

We take a five-minute break before the final scene, and I feel like this is the most important five-minute break of my life. Somehow, in these five minutes, I have to figure out how to be better at this than I've ever been at anything.

I look around for my mom, because she is the only one who can fix me at times like this, but I don't see her anywhere and I feel all alone. I glance over at Jordana, who has put her earbuds back in, and before I can turn away, she catches me looking at her and I feel like I am going to faint. I stare at the ground now and pray my mom gets back pronto.

I feel a tap on my shoulder, and it isn't a mom tap. Jordana sits down next to me.

"What's your name, again?" she asks.

"Jules," I say.

"I keep hearing that you're something special, but I'm not gonna lie. I don't get it."

"I know," I say. I want to cry because she has just told me I am not special, but I DO NOT cry.

"I mean, I'm sure you're great, but you're just so nervous all the time, and if they don't find the right girl for this Sylvie thing, we're all going to be out of work. So, how can I help?"

"I don't think I'm anything like Sylvie," I say.

"So what?" she says, and I really can't believe how this pretty southern accent can sound so mean coming out of Jordana's mouth. "That's the whole point of being an actress," she says. "You get to try on other people all the time. Do I seem like a bubbly, boy-crazy, empty-headed teenage girl to you?" she asks.

"I guess not," I say. "You're definitely not bubbly." I can't believe I say this, but it just comes out.

Jordana laughs, and I see that maybe she isn't always serious. "Want to know what I do before I have to perform?" she asks me.

"What?" I say.

"I try to get in the mood of my character, and I think Sydney is always in an empty-headed-teenager kind of mood." She takes one of her earbuds and sticks it in my ear. There is a very boy-crazy-teenager-type song on. I love this song. "What kind of mood do you think Sylvie is in?"

I shrug again, and wish I could stop shrugging and start knowing the right answers to things.

"I think Sylvie is in a get-up-and-dance-like-a-maniac-with-her-big-sister kind of mood. Don't you think so?" Jordana asks.

I think for a minute about what she said about trying on other people, and then I think about George's positive affirmawhatever-she-called-them, and I say, in a loud, clear Sylvie voice, "Okay, yeah!"

Jordana stands up, and I have to stand up with her or my earbud will fall out. "Come on, we're connected now. If I dance, you dance!" she says, hopping up and down and throwing her hands in the air to the music. I have no choice. I start to jump up and down, too, which makes me laugh, and all of a sudden I am belly-laughing and dancing and everyone is watching and I don't even care. I like it. I like this dancing-and-laughing-in-front-of-everyone person named Sylvie.

"Places!" I hear out of my empty ear.

We stop dancing and straighten our-selves out.

"Thanks, Jordana," I say.

"Sure," she says. "Now don't mess this up for me."

Moody is the word, all right. I look at my mom, who is finally back from the bath-room, and I don't feel nervous or alone anymore.

"Remember when you liked our old apart-ment?" Spencer asks Sydney and Sylvie.

"Oh, yeah, I just loved it," Sydney says. "Loved having to blow-dry my hair in the kitchen because we only had one bathroom. Oh, and I especially loved the mice!"

"Oh, yeah," Sylvie (me) says. "And you know what was the best part of all? Sharing a room with you and your powder-fresh feet. That was my favorite." Sarcasm. I did it!

Everyone giggles a little at this. Then I have to finish the whole scene by jumping on the kitchen counter and singing the words, "That was then, look at us now!" at the top of my lungs. Only, the first time I try to hoist myself up, I slide right back down and land on my bottom. Really hard. And it hurts. And it's in front of everyone. But I am not Jules right now, so I don't get upset. I do not have shaky knees, or butterflies, or a red-hot face. I just laugh so hard I actually snort (snort!) in front of everyone, and they all laugh, too.

"Take two!" I say in my loud Sylvie voice. And this time, I hoist myself right on up, and it feels like I'm in someone else's body. *Sylvie's body*, I think. And when I sing out those words at the top of my lungs, I throw my hands up in the air like a star, and then I look right at the camera and say, "Cha-cha-cha!" Everyone cheers, and I am very happy because I wasn't supposed to *cha-cha-cha*, the same way I wasn't supposed to *cha-cha-cha* at the Swish audition, and we all know how that turned out.

"There it is!" the director says now.

I look around. "There what is?" I ask.

"The star we've been looking for. Colby was right, you've got a lot of star power for a quiet little girl." Then he looks over at the person holding the big cards with our lines on them and says, "Add *cha-cha-cha* to the scene. That's a wrap for today, everybody."

This has been one of the best days of my whole life. My mom comes running over and gives me a big hug and she looks like she might cry, in a good way. "What happened? Where did that come from?" she asks me.

"From my moody big sister," I say, looking around for Jordana. She is already halfway out the door when I spot her. I want to thank her but there isn't time.

She just says, “See y’all Tuesday!” and she’s gone.

I turn to my mom. “Tuesday?”

“Don’t freak out,” she says. “They want to shoot the show for real Tuesday morning.”

“But the moving-up show . . .” I say.

“I’ve already told the director,” she says. “We are going to do our best to make it but, Jules, this is the business. You might have to miss it. It depends on how the shoot goes. Okay?”

“It couldn’t have been Field Day, huh?”

My mom laughs at this. “That sounds like something Sylvie would say.”

“It does, doesn’t it?”

acting your grade, tugging it out, and the right weather for boots

"How can I make Elinor less homesick?" I ask my parents early Monday morning. I haven't spoken to Elinor since Thursday. We didn't even run into her and her mom at hippo playground, since we spent the whole entire weekend doing restaurant-opening things and running errands, which doesn't ever feel at all like running. It should be called moving-like-snails-because-you-have-a-four-year-old-with-you errands.

"Just by being her friend," my mom says.

"And making new memories," my dad says. "But it takes a lot of time, Jules. You aren't going to be able to fix this one on your own."

I get nervous that Elinor made all kinds of new memories without me on Friday, and that she and Stinkytown have become best friends, and that Charlotte Stinkytown Pinkerton will be the reason Elinor is happy inside and out, all because I couldn't figure out that what she needs is new memories. Duh.

Right before I walk into the classroom, I stop and close my eyes. I picture Elinor and Charlotte all made up in shiny, fruity lip gloss and whispering secrets to each other about all of the funny things that happened in rehearsal on Friday. I open my eyes, hold my breath, and walk inside.

"Hi, Jules!" Elinor says when she sees me.

Phew! I think.

"How was it?" she asks.

"Yeah, tell us about your fake family," Teddy says.

"Well, they live in a mansion and they don't really have parents. Well, they do, but they aren't really on the show because they are celebrities and they drive all around the city in a car — like, to the movies in a car."

Teddy and Elinor laugh at this, and I am glad that they live in the same New York City I do.

"And I even have to get up on a kitchen counter and sing," I say.

"You are going to do that?" Teddy asks. "You, Jules Bloom? In front of everyone?"

"I already did it."

"Do it for us," Elinor says.

"Sure," I say. But I can't do it in front of them. It feels funny. I'm Jules in this classroom, not Sylvie. So, in a whisper-singing voice, I say, "That was then, look at us now!"

My friends are smiling at me.

"I'll believe it when I see it," Teddy says. I give him a small push.

"Hola, Jules," Ms. Leon says. "Welcome back."

"Hola," I say.

"We got a lot done on Friday, but I think if we just run through the show once, you'll do fine. But we have to hurry, because Field Day starts very soon!"

It is about 300 degrees outside, but they have not changed their minds about this Field Day idea.

"Okay, *vamos*!" Ms. Leon says. "Places!"

We all get up, and Ms. Leon shows me my spot and gives me the lines we worked on. I feel very bad that I might not be here for the real *espectáculo*, since I like the skits so much. But then I realize when I read my first line that my voice is still kind of shaky. I thought that all that acting I did last week would have fixed this problem.

"Weren't you acting in a TV show on Friday?" Charlotte asks. "I think we need a new narrator."

I feel like I might throw up.

"Charlotte," Ms. Leon says, "there is no excuse for that."

"Why not? Jules said I shouldn't be the music teacher when she knows I should be.

Even her own best friend knew Jules was wrong."

I am very mad at Charlotte, and very embarrassed, and very mad at Elinor all over again because she still doesn't know that the only reason I even cared about her part in the show was because I wanted her to hoot and holler and to just feel happy.

"I didn't say Jules was wrong," Elinor says. I forgive her right away.

"Okay, girls," Ms. Leon says. "Tomorrow is your moving-up play. How about we act like we are good and ready for third grade? How about Jules does the best job she can as narrator, and Charlotte does her best, and so on. That's all we can ask of each other."

"Fine," Charlotte says. "But —" Ms. Leon

just looks at her and she decides to stop talking.

I just nod my head and feel very left out for the whole rest of the rehearsal. I can't believe it, but I am glad when they blow the Field Day whistle over the loudspeaker and we go outside. Even Hippity Hopping in 300-degree heat feels better than being locked in a classroom with Stinkytown.

We are split into groups, and even though we are told that there are no winners or losers, and that we are just supposed to have fun, I am happy that Teddy and I are up against the ABC's in tug-of-war. Luckily, we have Lucas on our team, who is bigger than the usual second grader, and luckily, we have Teddy's brain on our team, who tells us Lucas should be in the way back. I look at Charlotte and stick my tongue out, and then I pray no one else saw me do this. Then she sticks her tongue out, and I don't know why but I think the whole thing is kind of funny.

All of this leads to me pulling the absolute hardest I have ever pulled on anything ever. Everyone is shouting and cheering, and my sneakers are slipping in the dirt, and I see the rope inching toward the ABC's, and I feel Teddy pulling ahead of me and

Lucas pulling behind me, and then all of a sudden, we pull so hard, the ABC's come flying toward us and we all end up in a heap. We won!

I start to cheer until I see that Charlotte is crying. She goes and sits under a tree and pulls her knees up to her chest. I start to walk over to her.

"She's probably going to say something mean," Teddy shouts as I walk.

"Maybe she will," I say.

"What do you want, Jules?" Charlotte asks with her head buried in her knees.

"How did you know it was me? You can't even see," I say.

"I can see your ridiculous high-tops through my legs. You are the only person who could be attached to those. Just like you are the only one who could be the narrator and you are the only one who gets to be an actress and you just get whatever you want."

"You get to be the music teacher and sing 'Do-Re-Mi.' I didn't know you wanted to be anything else," I say.

"It's not that," she says.

"Are you sad because you're moving to Long Island?" I ask.

She finally looks up at me. "We MIGHT be moving," she says. "And they didn't even ask me. They just drove us out there and started showing us houses with creepy basements, and Ella crawled all around every one of them, loving every second of it, and it's because she doesn't know that we belong here because she's only one year old, and you can't know that New York City is the best place when you're only one year old."

"No, I don't think you can," I say. I think of cute little Ella crawling all around and wish I was still friends with Charlotte just

so I could play with her. Charlotte probably started out cute, too.

I'm not sure what to say next, but I don't even have to think too much about it because Teddy comes running over and says, "You guys are not going to believe this. Look!"

We all look over to the big relay race everyone is cheering at, and we see that Elinor is way ahead of everyone, even the boys. She is running so fast and gets so far ahead that one of the boys just stops running and watches. When Elinor crosses the finish line, I am so excited for her, I start running. Teddy and Charlotte run over, too. We all jump up and down together, shouting, and even Elinor is hooting and hollering!

"I did NOT know you could run like that," I say. "Why didn't you tell me?"

"You never asked," she says.

"You beat everyone," Teddy says.

"I know," Elinor says. "Running is kind of my thing."

I am so happy that Elinor has a thing.

Everyone starts to walk toward the watermelon table, but I grab on to Elinor's shirt so she stays behind with me.

"What is it?" she asks.

"Are you happy now?" I ask.

"Sure," she says.

"Sometimes you don't look happy, and I

was thinking that maybe you're homesick or something."

Elinor looks down at her sneakers. "Maybe a little," she says.

"Well, I was thinking that maybe if we make a whole bunch of new memories together, the homesickness might go away a little," I say.

"Maybe it will," she says. "It went away a little just now, when I was running."

"That was my top secret project," I say. "That's why I forced you to be in the entertainers — to make you hoot and holler, so you would be happier."

Elinor looks at me funny. "And you thought being Maria von Trapp would do that?" she asks.

"Sorry about that," I say.

"It's okay," she says. "Besides, being in the show together will be a good memory. Even being in the show with Charlotte — she does make things memorable!"

We hold hands and walk over to the table with the giant watermelon slices on it, and I am happy Elinor is happy, but now I HAVE to make it to the show on time, or else this new memory will be one between Charlotte and Elinor, and I want it to be an all-of-us new memory. I try not to worry too much, since Teddy has started a seed-spitting contest and watermelon juice is flying everywhere as seeds soar through the hot air and land one by one in the dirt where our worm swimming pool used to be.

I smile at the memory of our worm swimming pool, and then I smile because even Charlotte is spitting her seeds with us now. But she never says one word to any of us, which isn't so bad, since it means no one says anything mean the whole rest of the day.

On the way home, I feel so over-hot that even the bus air-conditioning doesn't help. I feel like I can't take it for one more minute, and neither can the city.

"Watch," my mom says. "The heavens are going to open up the minute we get off of this bus." We are on the way home and the sky is almost black.

"Is it nighttime already?" Big Henry asks.

"It isn't nighttime," I say. "There is going to be a big storm. Look. Here it comes!" And when we step off the bus, the rain comes down on us so hard we are soaked before we start running. My mom grabs our hands.

"Here we go!" she shouts, and we run as fast as we can to the corner and toward our building. There isn't anything more real-life than running around New York City in the pouring rain.

We get into the lobby and look at each other as we catch our breath. "It's a good thing I was wearing my boots," my little brother says. I look down at my soaked turquoise-and-pink high-top sneakers and start laughing.

"You've been waiting awhile to say that, huh, Hank?" I ask.

"I'll tell you who's been waiting awhile," a voice comes from behind us, and it makes me scream at the top of my lungs. The great Grandma Gilda is waiting for us and I forgot all about it.

"George!" I run over to her and give her a sopping-wet hug.

Big Henry screams, too, and almost knocks us all over with his running hug.

"I used a positive whatever-you-call-it yesterday!" I say.

"Affirmation!" George says. "Did it work?"

"Yep," I say.

"Good, let's do one now to see if it helps me get up out of this chair."

Upstairs, we get into dry clothes and Big Henry tells her all about school and his scooter, which he rides better than he walks. And I tell her all about *Look at Us Now!* and my TV family, and Elinor and my side project. After dinner and a big-time scooter race around the kitchen island, it is time for me to read over my lines one more time.

I have to wake up very early to get to the set, since there will be makeup! And hairstyling! And wardrobe! *Wardrobe* means they give you outfits to wear that you would never really wear, but that are very, very cool. I. Can't. Wait.

"Hey, Eddie," George whispers at my door, and nods her head in the direction of my roommate. "Is he asleep?"

I nod. Big Henry fell asleep as soon as he pushed PLAY on Paddington.

"You didn't say anything about Charlotte," George says.

"She's just . . . Charlotte," I say. "But I am trying to be a little bit nice to her since she is moving and then I won't have to see her anymore."

“I thought you were wishing you might be able to see her basement,” George says.

“I was. I am. I don’t know. Charlotte is confusing,” I say.

“Most people are,” George says. “If they weren’t, they’d be boring.”

I think about this after she gives me a giganto Grandma Gilda squeeze. I think about how my mom made that game show to show me how life isn’t boring. Now, I kind of wish it *was* boring.

lost-and-found voices, two shows for the price of one, and nowadays illnesses

My mom wakes me up with a kiss on the head.

"I just want one tiny moment of calm before we go," she says.

"I have to make it to school in time," I say.

"Listen, Jules. I am willing to do just about anything for you. I've taken off from work, I've let you miss some school, and Daddy and I have already put a lot into this because it seems like it's important to you, and because we actually think you're good at it."

"You do?"

"We do," she says. "When I saw you get up on that countertop, I realized that this might not be just a regular after-school activity."

"Me, too," I say, even though I hadn't really thought about it that way until right this minute.

"But —" my mom says, and I know this *but* is going to be a big one. "But watching you put all this pressure on yourself to do everything makes me a little nervous."

"You never get nervous," I say.

"I'm nervous about this," she says.

"Well, I can handle it," I say. "Just like you. You do everything for everyone and you work and you make game shows and you make dinner," I say.

"I don't make dinner well. Not like Daddy," she says.

"Well, that's okay, because then you would be perfect, and nobody's perfect."

She smiles.

"I can do both things," I say.

"Okay," she says. "Let's see what the day brings."

And the morning race begins. The whole

family is coming to the set — even Big Henry gets to miss school to come to the taping, and he is very excited.

We eat bagels and drink juice while a man does my hair, and Big Henry asks 350 questions about everything. "Why is this camera here?" "What if this camera doesn't work?" "How does Jules know what to say?" "Why is Jules named Sylvie now?" "Can my name be Han Solo now?" And on and on and on. The only good thing about all his question-asking is that he makes me laugh a lot.

“Ready?” my dad asks.

“Yep,” I say. I am proud that I do not shrug.

And then all of a sudden, “ACTION!”

The rest of the morning goes by in a flash. I work really hard and I try not to think about missing the show, because it makes me feel horribly sad to think that I would miss my first memory with Elinor. This is what I am thinking when my dad comes over during a break.

“You know, I was thinking,” he says. “You’ve been making memories with Elinor since the day you met her. Digging for worms, handstand contests, the not-Swish-girl party . . . So I don’t think you have to worry so much about this one show."

"Those are just small moments," I explain to my dad. "What Elinor needs is a big, momentous memory that will make her want to stay forever and ever."

"I see," he says. "Big."

"Momentous," I say.

"Got it," he says.

The break is over, and at last the final scene comes, and I am excited. I think I am probably going to have to hop up on that counter and sing at least five times, since it is the last scene and all the scenes need at least a few takes. But we do it in one take! One take! I think I am better at being Sylvie than I am at being myself.

"That's a wrap!" the director yells, and butterflies feel like they are going to fly out of my mouth like a capful of orange Swish Mouthwash.

My dad and Grandma Gilda hoot and holler as I come over to them, and I feel shy about this. No one else on the show has a group of people hooting and hollering.

"Let's go," I say, and I am pulling on my mom's arm like a two-year-old.

Our cab makes it almost all the way back uptown very quickly, and I am sure we will make it until we end up in the biggest traffic jam I have ever seen. I throw my head back against the seat.

"Jules!" my dad says. "Settle down." Then

he sticks his head way out the window to see what's happening out there. He turns back to us. "Well, who's up for making a run for it?"

"I am!" I say. Then my mom, my dad, and I agree to meet George and Hank there. Thank goodness all the rain cooled off the air a little because the three of us run the fastest I have ever run. I am laughing as I go, watching my dad dodge ladies with baby strollers and jump over dog leashes.

When we finally get to school, I am sweating, but I don't stop. I walk-run right toward the multipurpose room, where my whole class is lined up in the hallway.

"Jules!" Elinor runs over to me and gives me a big hug. "You made it! Guess what —

Charlotte had the great idea that I should wear running clothes and actually run while I sing 'Fa — a long, long way to run!' Isn't that clever?"

"It is!" I say. It is.

"Julesium, your face is melting," Teddy says.

I touch my sweaty face and look at my mom. "It is kind of melting, honey. We should have taken off that makeup."

"Can we clean up in the bathroom?" I ask Ms. Leon.

"There really isn't time."

My mom dabs my face. "Aren't you going to freak out about melting?" she asks.

"Nope," I say.

"Are you going to throw up?" Teddy asks.

"Nope," I say.

"Okay, see you inside," my dad says, kissing me on the head.

We start to walk in and I tap Charlotte on the shoulder. "What?" she whisper-yells.

"I just wanted to say that I think basements are magical," I say.

Charlotte smiles at this, and in we go! Even when I see the rows and rows of parents and grandparents, I don't freak out. My legs don't shake. I don't even care that I probably look like a sweaty circus clown. Then, when I see Grandma Gilda and Big Henry sneak into the room, I feel even better. Each group talks about their small moments, and the entertainers group sings about their small moment, and I realize for the first time that Charlotte has a very pretty singing voice and that Elinor does not, but at least she looks happy. And I am happy and lost in my own head until I hear Teddy start talking.

"As scientists, we learned about plants, and we also learned that anything orange makes Jules throw up."

I stare at Teddy so hard, and all he does is shrug at me. The whole class laughs at this, and I hear Big Henry say really loud, "Teddy said Jules frows up!"

I wait until the room calms down to say the final narrator line. "And I learned that we made a lot of small moments together in our classroom community," I say. "And that we wouldn't have learned anything without our mayor!" Ms. Leon laughs a little because I surprised her with this line.

Then we all start singing "So Long, Farewell," and I look at my friends down the line and I can't believe this day is about to be over. I also can't believe that Charlotte's face is sprouting giant red blotches as she goes, and I wonder for a second if she is nervous or something. We all bow and everyone claps very loudly, like they did at the taping this morning, except this feels even better.

My dad runs over with his camera and we pose for a class picture, and Teddy, Elinor, Charlotte, and I line up next to each other and smile.

"What's wrong with Charlotte's face?" Big Henry asks this so loud that the smiling picture turns into a laughing picture, which my dad shows us right away. There I am

with my sweaty clown makeup, and there Charlotte is with her splotchy-strawberry face, and there is Teddy pretending to throw up all over the place, and there is Elinor throwing her head back laughing and looking really, really happy. Happy on the inside.

"I remember when you all posed for your nursery-school picture," my mom says.

Something comes over me, and I start to sing. "That was then," floats out of my mouth, and then I hop up on a chair and sing, "Look at us now!!!!"

"It's scarlet fever," my mom says. She has just hung up the phone and come into the bedroom, where Elinor and I are standing on our heads against my bed, since I'm still too tired from yesterday to stand on my hands.

I gasp and look at Elinor. She seems surprised, too.

The only other time in my life I have ever heard about scarlet fever was in the movie *The Miracle Worker,* and when little baby Helen Keller gets scarlet fever, she can't see or hear ever again! I think of all the awful things I've said about Charlotte and all the times I've wished she weren't even around. I feel terrible.

"I didn't even know a nowadays person could get scarlet fever!" I say.

"Relax, Jules," my mom says. "It's not like it used to be, thanks to modern medicine. It's just like strep. Only more . . . dramatic. Charlotte will be fine now that she's on antibiotics."

"Well, thank goodness," Elinor says.

"Yes, thank goodness," I say, since I forgot to say this right away. Then I think, *Now I don't have to feel bad that I was feeling a little bit happy about Charlotte moving to Long Island.*

"And they aren't moving," my mom says.

I gasp again.

"At least, not this year," she says. "Good?"

"Great!" I say, thinking fast. I'm sure this is what I am supposed to say since just a minute ago I was worried Charlotte might not even live to see third grade. But what I am really thinking (sarcastically) is, *Third grade with Stinkytown? Just what I always wanted.*

"I think *scarlet fever* sounds glamorous," Elinor says as the phone rings again and my mom rushes to pick it up.

"I think it sounds dangerous," I say.

"Jules!" Big Henry crashes in on us again, and again we fall over on top of each other.

"Big Henry!" I say.

"Colby Kingston says Rick Hinkley's leg

isn't as cracked up as it was in the first place," he says.

Elinor and I run to the kitchen, and my mom's finger is already in place, like it was waiting for us to interrupt.

She hangs up.

"Just when I thought we were going to have a nice little break," my mom says.

"What?" Elinor and I say at the same exact time.

"Jinx!" Big Henry says.

"Turns out being part hockey star really *does* help. He's ready to go, starting in three weeks. What do you think?" she asks.

We only have a week left of school, I think. I am silent.

"Jules?" she says.

I say nothing.

"Elinor?" she says.

Elinor keeps her mouth closed, but shouts something behind her cheeks.

"Oh!" my mom says. "Big Henry, release the jinx!"

"Jules and Elinor, Jules and Elinor, Jules and Elinor!" Big Henry says.

Elinor and I explode with screams.

"Is it enough time?" my mom asks.

"It's the perfect amount of time," I say. *Just enough time for me to turn back into a spy-girl*, I think. I even get two weeks of vacation in between.

"Maybe I can think of a side project!" I say.

Then we all hoot and holler for a good long time.

For a sneak peek at Jules's next starring role, turn the page!

★★★

STARRING Jules

(SUPER-SECRET SPY GIRL)

"They say your movie is going to be a blockbuster," Charlotte says the minute she sees me.

"Who says?" I say.

"*Variety*," Charlotte says.

"What's *Variety*?" I ask.

"It's a magazine all about important things that happen in show business," Charlotte says. "I can't believe you don't read it. You are seriously the worst child actress ever."

"Well, maybe Jules doesn't NEED a magazine to tell her things she already knows," Elinor says, "because she's an actual actress in an actual movie, so she already knows these things in the first place." What am I ever going to do without Elinor this summer?

"Well, anyway, between Rick Hinkley and Emma Saxony, who is practically perfect, I don't think anyone will notice you so much, Jules, so that's good," Charlotte says. "You won't have to be so crazy nervous all the time."

I glare at her because I'm pretty sure she isn't complimenting me.

ACKNOWLEDGMENTS

If I absolutely *had* to do second grade all over again, I would want the following people to be in my class: Rhonda Penn Seidman, because even though we actually could have been in the same second-grade class, no one would ever let us be, and because I would have been a much happier second grader with her than without her; Denise Goldman, because she would make me belly-laugh and feel confident all at once (and then she would make me do jumping jacks); Amy Flisser, because she would read even my worst lists and tell me they moved her; Chava Ortner, because she would help me check things off my list and tell me not to be so hard on my second-grade self; and Jon Ain, because I think we would have been good for each other even at seven.

So much love and gratitude to Gail Levine, Chuck Levine, Michael Levine, Meryl and Stewart Ain, and Richard Seidel (for letting a certain second grader write her first story on his newfangled computer); to Diana Berrent (for her magic-making photography and for her friendship); to the teachers and administrators at Manorhaven Elementary School in Port Washington, NY; to the exceptional Jill Grinberg and everyone at Jill Grinberg Literary Management; to Jenne Abramowitz (for truly getting me and for reining me in — all at once!); and to Grace and Elijah — my kids, my muses, my absolute favorite people in the world.

BETH AIN was raised in Allentown, PA, but fell in love with New York City, where she lived until recently and where she tried her hand at raising two kids, an experience that gave her some good lessons in what makes city kids (and city moms) tick. Enter Jules Bloom — lover of all things Upper West Side. In search of wide-open spaces, Beth headed for the hills of Port Washington, Long Island, where she, her husband, and their two kids have fallen in love all over again. This time with small-town life, where thankfully, she can see the Empire State Building from Main Street, which makes it pretty easy to imagine what Jules is up to.